Moo Moo Cha Cha

Author: David Mack

Illustrator: Sarah Miller

Editors: Jenny Dunn & Sarah Miller

ACKNOWLEDGEMENTS

We would like to thank Carlos, for his help in translating this story to Spanish.
We would also like to thank John, for his help in digitizing these illustrations.

ISBN: 0692927573
ISBN-13: 978-0692927571

Library of Congress Control Number: 2018911318

DEDICATION

This book is dedicated to my kids, who have enriched my life and probably shortened it as well. To Devon, Emilio (Mano), Paige, and Alexander (Xander), Gin and I wish you a long and happy life.
– D. A. M.

Ava, Oliver, and Ava's grandparents: thank you for supporting Mama's many evenings and weekends of *Moo Moo Cha Cha*. It started when you were a mere twinkle, Ava, and finally done once you could see those cows dance yourself.
– S. H. M.

To my Munchkin, Sierra. Remember, you'll miss 100% of the shots you don't take. Don't let anyone tell you that you can't accomplish whatever you set your mind to.
– J. K. D.

It was a beautiful day on the Mack Farm.
Everyone was enjoying the day, including the cows!

Suddenly, music filled the farm!

"This music makes me want to dance!" said Fresa.

At first the other cows were curious.

One of the cows asked, "Fresa, what are you doing?"

Farmer Mack said, "Hmm, the milk is a bit different today."

The next day, Fresa heard another fun song
coming from the Mack family farmhouse.

"Join me! The music is so good. You can dance just like me!"

Paige asked, "Hey, Dad, have you figured out
why the milk is a little different?"

Well, the next day the music kept playing,
and Fresa kept dancing.

The other cows saw how much fun Fresa was
having and joined in. "Isn't this wonderful?
It's so much fun to dance together!"

Now the milk was *really* different.
"What is going on?" asked Farmer Mack.

The next morning, Farmer Mack saw the cows dancing.
He realized it was changing the milk!

Farmer Mack shouted, "STOP! STOP! NO! NO!
You are shaking up the milk!"

Later, Farmer Fralin stopped by for a visit. Farmer Mack explained, "I had to stop the cows from dancing. They were shaking the milk and making it taste different."

"Oh really?" asked Farmer Fralin.
"Do you mind if I try some?"

"Farmer Mack, this is delicious! It *IS* different than regular milk, but it is really good. I would drink this anytime."

Farmer Fralin said, "I think you could sell this after all!
Add a bit of chocolate or fresh strawberries too!
Just keep those cows happy. Let them dance!"

Farmer Mack apologized. "I should have let you dance! I love what you did to the milk! We are going to call it a *milkshake.*"

"Have fun! Turn up the music!"

So Fresa and the other cows went back to dancing. They called their dance the *Moo Moo Cha Cha.*

The Mack family opened a milkshake stand
named after the cows' dance.

People lined up day after day for the
Moo Moo Cha Cha milkshakes. Their cool
sweetness was perfect in the summer heat.

And every night the cows would fall asleep under dancing stars, dreaming of doing the *Moo Moo Cha Cha*.

ORIGIN STORY

The idea behind this book came from a chance encounter at a restaurant. They had a dish on the menu called "Moo Moo Cha Cha" and my inner voice said, 'that sounds like a good kids' book name.' Then I started making up the story to go with the name and amusing myself. I spent half that lunch dreaming up the story instead of talking to friends. By the time lunch was over, I thought to myself that I had a pretty good story. A few weeks later I saw a flyer someone had drawn and I loved it. The drawing was in a whimsical, fun style and I wondered who created it. I asked around and it turns out that Sarah had drawn it. I told her the book idea and she loved it. There was one more friend that I shared the idea with and she loved it as much as Sarah and I. Jenny was truly a driving force to get the book done, and she was always super excited to work on the book. It was fun working with them both and I hope you enjoy the book as much as we did creating it.

-David Mack, 2018

CPSIA information can be obtained
at www.ICGtesting.com
Printed in the USA
LVHW071632220219
608478LV00013B/190/P

* 9 7 8 0 6 9 2 9 2 7 5 7 1 *